Magic Pony

Ghost
in the House

For Kiran

No part of this publication may be reproduced, stored in a retrieval system, or transmitted in any form or by any means, electronic, mechanical, photocopying, recording, or otherwise, without written permission of the publisher. For information regarding permission, write to Scholastic Ltd., Euston House, 24 Eversholt Street, London NW1 1DB, United Kingdom.

ISBN 978-0-545-21321-9

All rights reserved. Published by Scholastic Inc., 557 Broadway, New York, NY 10012, by arrangement with Scholastic Ltd. SCHOLASTIC, APPLE PAPERBACKS, and associated logos are trademarks and/or registered trademarks of Scholastic Inc.

12 11 10 9 8 7 6 5 4   11 12 13 14 15/0

Printed in the U.S.A.   40
This edition first printing, July 2010

Magic Pony

Ghost in the House

Elizabeth Lindsay
Illustrated by John Eastwood

SCHOLASTIC INC.

New York   Toronto   London   Auckland
Sydney   Mexico City   New Delhi   Hong Kong

Chapter 1

Poor Penelope

Annie was in the kitchen, opening a sardine can so she could give Tabitha her special Saturday pussycat breakfast. This morning, the toaster had refused to work and, before staggering outside with a pile of laundry to hang up, Mom had explained that you can leave a toaster to work on its own, but bread under a broiler needs watching. On the broiler pan, four slices of well-browned toast were reaching a point way beyond done. The sardine smell had Tabitha winding herself eagerly around Annie's legs and purring loudly, and the smell of burning toast had Annie diving to the rescue.

There was a knock at the front door.

"Somebody's at the door!" Dad shouted

from the living room as he unscrewed another tiny part from the broken toaster. In her panic to save the toast Annie didn't hear — she was too busy switching off the broiler and blowing on the burned pieces.

"*Meow*," said Tabitha as a reminder.

"Coming."

Annie put down the broiler pan, grabbed a fork, and dug out the sardines. Tabitha stretched up and, shoving her nose into the bowl as soon as she could, dived in.

There was another, louder knock.

"Somebody please answer the door," shouted Dad. Jamie's footsteps clattered down the stairs and clumped across the hall. "Thank goodness someone's going." Another screw joined the collection on a plate.

"I burned the toast."

"I know. I can smell it." The hall door opened and Jamie came in. "Who is it?" Dad asked.

"Mr. Potter! He didn't stop. He asked me to give this letter to Annie." Jamie held out a pink envelope.

"What letter?" asked Annie, darting to look.

In typical brotherly fashion, Jamie sent the letter spinning across the room. Too curious to complain, Annie caught it.

"I know what's in it and I told Mr. Potter you would," said Jamie.

Annie looked at the envelope. Her name was printed in bold black letters and underlined. "Penelope typed it on her new computer."

"Well, aren't you going to open it?"

"I am," said Annie, skipping across the room. "Upstairs."

"What about the toast?" cried Dad.

"Jamie can do it."

"That's not fair," objected Jamie. But he was too late. Annie was gone.

Once in her bedroom, Annie pushed the door closed and sat on her bed. Then she looked up at the pony poster above her

chest of drawers. The head of a handsome chestnut pony stared down at her.

"Ned," said Annie. "This is a letter from Penelope Potter. Why do you think she's writing to me?" Annie waited, hoping for a reply, but none came. The pony in the poster remained a picture. "Please magic, please work today," wished Annie. "Make Ned come alive." Annie jumped from the bed. Her three china ponies, Esmerelda, Prince, and Percy, were looking out of the window. She looked out, too. But this morning the field across the lane

was empty. Annie tore open the envelope and pulled out a pink sheet of paper.

"It's even got a pony logo," she said. "I'll read it to you. Then maybe you'll come alive. We could have an amazing magic pony adventure all day if you did." She looked longingly up at Ned, remembering her first glimpse of him in the window of Cosby's Magic Emporium, the shop where Jamie bought his magic tricks. Had Mr. Cosby known all along

that Ned's poster was magic? Did he know that the pony in the picture came alive, and that sometimes he might be actual pony size and sometimes as tiny as Percy, the smallest of her china horses? Annie was sure that no other pony poster in the whole world was so special or such

Dear Annie,

I was sick in the night and now I feel yucky. Today I was going to a horse show, but Mommy says I have to rest. Pebbles is in his stable. He needs feeding (half a scoopful of pony nuts) and exercise (halter in tack room). Then his stable needs mucking out. Tell my dad if you can't and he'll have to do it. But I know I can count on you.

From a suffering friend,

Penelope Potter

P.S. When you've finished, come straight to the house and tell me how Pebbles is.

a secret. She smoothed out the letter and cleared her throat.

"Oh, yes," cried Annie, flinging her window wide. By leaning out she could just see into Penelope's little stable yard. There was Pebbles, head out over his stable door, waiting for his breakfast. "I must go at once. See you later, Ned."

Then, not bothering to close the window, Annie raced for the door. The

pony in the poster turned ever so slightly to watch her go.

Downstairs, Annie burst into the living room.

"I'm going to look after Pebbles," she informed everyone.

"I knew she would," said Jamie.

"Not before breakfast," said Dad, lifting

the plate with all the toaster parts and putting it on top of the television.

"There is no breakfast," said Annie. "I burned it."

"And I've made some more," called Mom from the kitchen. "Toast is on its way. Put on your boots if you're going to muck out. I don't want manure all over your sneakers. You can take your toast with you if you're in such a rush."

"Thanks, Mom," said Annie, running into the kitchen to find her boots.

"What do you want on it?"

"Honey, please." Annie pulled off her sneakers and crammed her feet into her rubber boots. She took the offered toast.

"Here," said Mom. "You can give Pebbles these with my compliments." And she handed Annie a paper bag. Annie shook it. "Carrot sticks," explained Mom. "Nice long ones so he won't choke. You can add them to his pony nuts. And give Penelope my love when you go and see her. Tell her I hope she gets better soon."

"I will," said Annie and, with the toast between her teeth, she flung open the back door, hurried across the grass, and around the house to the side gate.

Chapter 2

Looking After Pebbles

Once on the road, Annie set off purposefully toward Penelope's stable. This was the first time she had ever looked after Pebbles all by herself and she was really excited. It made up for her disappointment that Ned's magic was not working today. She chewed her toast, hardly noticing that she was eating. By the time she reached the stable yard gate, there was only the crust left. She held it between her teeth while she undid the latch.

A long, low whicker came from Pebbles's stable.

"I know, I know. You're saying, 'where's my breakfast?'" Annie held out her hand, fingers flat, balancing the toast crust.

Pebbles's lips wobbled open and the crust was gone. He crunched happily while Annie stroked his dappled gray neck and looked in the stable. "Not a wisp of hay left. No wonder you're hungry." Smelling the carrots, Pebbles pushed at the paper bag. "No! You can have the carrots with your breakfast. I'll get it now."

Annie ran to the tack room and opened the door. She was greeted by the inviting smell of leather, saddle soap, and pony. Lifting the lid of the feed bin, she measured half a scoopful of pony nuts into a bucket and shook the carrot sticks on top.

As Annie left the tack room, another long, low whicker greeted her, and Pebbles, with ears pricked, stretched his neck toward his breakfast. Annie held the bucket behind her as she undid the stable door.

"Back, Pebbles," she commanded and the pony stepped politely out of the way. But the moment she put down the bucket, his head was in it. Annie shut the door and smiled. "Breakfast at last, eh boy?"

"Yoo-hoo, Annie!"

Annie turned to find Mrs. Plumley, their neighbor from next door, beaming at her from the gate, and Ruddles, Mrs. Plumley's dog, wagging his tail.

"Hello, Mrs. Plumley," said Annie, skipping over. "Hello, Ruddles." Annie bent down as the little dog pulled against his leash to say hello. She gave him a big cuddle and Ruddles gave her a big lick. "Oh, help," she cried. "Right on the nose."

"He doesn't mind noses, Annie." Mrs.

Plumley chuckled. "He gives all his friends big doggy kisses, don't you Ruddles?"

"*Woof, woof,*" barked Ruddles in agreement.

"Now where's young Penelope this morning? Her mom told me she was off to a horse show today."

"She's not feeling very well," said Annie. "So I'm looking after Pebbles."

"Oh, dear. I'm sorry she's sick," said Mrs. Plumley. "Well, when you see her, you tell her from me to get better soon. And that I'm glad to see she's got a friend for Pebbles at last."

"What sort of a friend?"

"A pony friend, of course. I knew by the chestnut color it wasn't Pebbles. Now that's nice, I thought."

Annie's heart skipped a beat and she hoped that, just maybe, Ned's magic was working and he had come out of his picture. She raced across the yard to look. She even climbed to the top of the gate to make herself higher, but there was no pony in Pebbles's field.

"There isn't a pony there," said Annie, trying not to sound disappointed.

"Well, now. I could have sworn I saw one grazing over by Penelope's blue barrel jumps," Mrs. Plumley said. "But there you are, dear. It's my eyes playing tricks again. And truth is, I wasn't wearing my glasses. Come along Ruddles, we must leave Annie and get along. We're off to do our shopping."

"Bye, Mrs. Plumley."

"Bye-bye, Annie dear. Come by and see us soon."

With a wave, Mrs. Plumley and Ruddles

continued on down the street toward the main road. Annie longed to groom Pebbles's dappled coat, but the pony was looking expectantly from his stable and she knew he wanted to go into his field. Annie ran to the tack room and, putting the hoof pick in her pocket, grabbed the halter. Back in the stable, she slipped the halter on and tied Pebbles to the rope on the hitching ring. Then, carefully lifting each foot, she picked out the dirt with the hoof pick.

"There," she said. "All done." Untying the halter rope, she led Pebbles out of his stable and across the yard to the field gate. Once he was free, Pebbles bucked four times and cantered off. Annie admired his mane and tail streaming in the breeze before she carefully fastened the gate. Now she had the stable to clean.

Penelope often let her muck out, so she knew the routine. She collected the pitchfork and wheelbarrow, then got started. By the time she wheeled the full barrow to the manure heap, Pebbles was grazing quietly. To her disappointment, there was no sign of a chestnut pony grazing with him. Mrs. Plumley's eyes certainly had been playing tricks on her.

Annie swept the yard, rinsed out Pebbles's food bucket, then put away the broom, wheelbarrow, and pitchfork. By the time Mr. Potter drove down the driveway from Penelope's house, across the street, and into the yard, everything was neat and clean.

"Thanks for doing all that," he said from the car. "Penelope says to go and see her. I've just picked up Trudi. So between the pair of you, you should manage to cheer her up, poor thing. She's upset about missing her show jumping."

"Who wouldn't be?" Annie sighed to herself, wishing she could do show jumping, too. To Mr. Potter she said, "All right. I'll go and see her now."

"That's my girl," said Mr. Potter. "Now Penelope and Trudi want Wally Whizzer Wonderstick Ice Cream. What would you like?"

"Me?" said Annie, surprised to be asked. "I'll have the same, please."

"Since I've got to drive all the way to the supermarket, I'll get a boxful."

"A boxful." Annie gasped as Mr. Potter backed out of the yard and drove off toward the main road. Annie only had a Wally Whizzer Wonderstick Ice Cream on very special occasions. Maybe this was turning into one?

Trudi was Penelope's best friend and if she was at the house, Penelope must be feeling better. I just hope they don't gang up on me like they do on the school bus, Annie thought.

She admired Pebbles's clean straw bed, his fresh bucket of water, and bursting hay net for the last time and closed the stable door. Perhaps this afternoon Penelope might be well enough to take Pebbles for a ride and would let her do some grooming after all. She hung up the halter and hoof pick in the tack room and cast an eye round the little stable yard.

"Extremely neat and clean, Annie. Well done!" The unexpected voice made Annie jump and she spun around. To her astonishment a chestnut pony leaned out over Pebbles's stable door. "The only problem is you've locked me in."

"Ned," cried Annie. "Ned!" And she rushed to fling her arms around the chestnut pony's neck. "I didn't think the magic would happen today."

"Well it did and here I am," said the pony. "Will you please let me out?" Annie undid the bolt and opened the door. Ned pranced into the yard. "I see Penelope's got you busy as usual. Cleaning and sweeping and so on. You've certainly done a good job."

"Penelope's not feeling well."

"I know," said Ned. "You told me. And as you're on your way to visit her, I'll come, too."

"But what if somebody sees you?"

"Let me worry about that." He gave Annie a gentle nudge with his nose. "After all, you didn't see me go into the stable, did you now?"

"You must have been your tiny self, that's why. But Mrs. Plumley saw you in the field."

"True. I was a little careless, but it was good to get a few mouthfuls of fresh grass."

"Well, please don't be careless again," cautioned Annie.

"There's no need to worry about me. Just lead the way to Penelope."

Chapter 3

Three's a Crowd

Annie pushed away all her worries. It was good to have Ned walking at her side as she crossed the street from the stable yard into Penelope's back driveway. Annie's boots and four pony feet crunched along the gravel until they came into the yard.

"Once upon a time, long ago, these

garages were stables," said Annie, pointing to three garage doors. "Just imagine having horses in your backyard."

"Well," said Ned. "I don't think that's as good as having one in your bedroom."

"I was forgetting that." Annie laughed. She became suddenly serious. "I can't knock on the door until you are your tiny self, Ned. If Mrs. Potter sees you, she'll be furious. Ponies aren't allowed in the yard."

But Annie didn't have a chance to knock. There were two impatient barks from inside the house and the back door opened. She jumped in front of Ned and stretched her arms wide as if by doing so she could block him from view and riveted her gaze to the face that looked down at her. It was Mrs. Potter, clutching a fluffy, coffee-colored poodle.

"There you are at last, Annie," she said and, gazing down at Annie's startled face, she asked, "What's the matter?"

"I, uh . . . !" Annie glanced over her shoulder. Ned had vanished. "Nothing." She lowered her arms sheepishly. "I didn't know you had a dog."

"I don't. Penelope's looking after Pom Pom for her Aunt Diana."

"He's very pretty."

"I suppose he is if you like dogs." Mrs. Potter sniffed. "Take your boots off and leave them on the newspaper by the washing machine. Penelope and Trudi are in the TV room. They're expecting you. Since Penelope's sick, I'm taking Pom Pom out for his walk."

Annie obediently pulled off her boots and stepped into the utility room. The door to the kitchen was open. Compared to her house, Penelope's house was like a palace, the rooms were so big. She plopped her boots on the first convenient piece of newspaper.

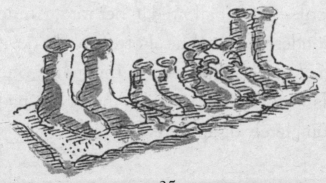

"Good-bye," said Mrs. Potter, and she pulled the back door closed behind her, just missing the tiny chestnut pony galloping across the doormat on his way to the kitchen.

"Ned," whispered Annie. "Wait for me."

Annie skidded across the slippery floor tiles, past a stove, a fridge, a freezer, and a row of gleaming kitchen gadgets. As ponies weren't allowed in her yard, Annie wondered what Mrs. Potter would do if she knew she had one in the house. She glanced under the table but Ned had completely disappeared.

She peeped around the door into the hall and was met by a strong lavender smell, even though the flower vase on the hall table was empty. Polish, Annie guessed. The wooden floor shone and, dotted here and there like giant stepping stones, were an array of throw rugs. Annie

resisted the temptation to go skating on her socks and tiptoed to what she thought was the TV room door. As she hardly ever came into Penelope's house, she hoped she'd remembered it correctly.

She took a quick look around, wondering where Ned could have gone, then pushed the door open. The room was in semidarkness, but she could make out the television and the heavy curtains covering the windows. Leaving the door ajar, she went inside and her toes met the softness of a thick pile carpet. She expected Penelope to be lying down, but tiptoeing forward she could see that the sofa in front of the television was empty. The door slammed.

"Whoo, whooo, whooooo!" A wailing voice was behind her. Before she could turn, she was enveloped by a big cloth. Hands grasped and twirled her and she couldn't do anything but spin. Stumbling, she tripped and was pushed onto the sofa, banging her elbow. She heard girls' shrieks and then they closed in and wriggling fingers tickled her.

"We are the ghosts of the house!" Penelope was instantly recognizable.

"Get off me," Annie shouted.

"We have come to haunt youoooooooo!" Trudi's unmistakable high-pitched tones joined in. Annie wriggled away in a fury and rolled across the floor. Struggling to

free herself, she managed to pull off what turned out to be a bedspread. She sat down in front of the television nursing her aching arm, her face a furious pink.

"No need to look so mad," said Penelope. "We wanted to give you a surprise, that's all."

"A tiny little scare," said Trudi, with one of her pretend smiles. "We got the idea from the ghost video we were watching."

"And now we'll open the curtains," said Penelope. "Can you do it, Trude — I feel all weak and wobbly."

Still seething, Annie struggled to her feet, but she wasn't going to give them the pleasure of seeing how upset she was. Secretly, she rubbed her elbow.

"I just came to tell you about Pebbles," she said. "I thought you were sick."

"I am," said Penelope, flopping back onto a pile of cushions. "Too sick to go out, too sick to do anything much." Trudi swished open the tall curtains and a stream of sunlight flooded the room. "Not that wide," said Penelope. "We'll never be able to see the video with that much light."

She turned wide-eyed toward Annie and put on a trembly voice. "We're watching *Hullabaloo and the Haunting of Flintstone Castle*. Really spooky."

"I'm not staying to see that," said Annie, realizing that, as usual, they were ganging up on her. "I've got things to do."

Before she could reach the door, Trudi beat her to it and stood barring the way with an oily grin on her face.

"But you haven't told Penelope anything about Pebbles. How does she know if you looked after him properly?"

"If she doesn't believe I did, she can check for herself," said Annie, refusing to be intimidated.

"Oh, Annie, don't go," said Penelope. "I do want to know how Pebbles is. Please come and tell me. And Daddy's bringing you a Wally Whizzer Wonderstick. You can't go until you've had that." Annie sighed. She had to admit she was tempted by the Wally Whizzer.

"Oh, all right. But no playing around." She sat next to Penelope.

"So how is Pebbles?"

"Yes, how is Pebbles?" repeated Trudi, leaning over the back of the sofa and staring straight into Annie's face.

"Did you give him his breakfast?" Penelope asked.

"Yes, did you give him his breakfast?" repeated Trudi. Then, with a sudden lunge, Penelope pulled out a can from behind a cushion and Trudi took one out from behind her back. They took aim and fired. Annie jumped out of the way, but it was too late to stop herself from being showered in Rainbow Sticky Foam.

"You're mean, both of you!" she cried. "This stuff takes forever to get off."

"Now, now, Annie," said Penelope, falling onto her cushions and shaking with laughter. "Can't you take a joke?"

"No sense of humor," said Trudi, flouncing around the sofa to sit beside her friend. "I don't know why you asked her to look after Pebbles. He deserves someone much nicer."

"Don't be mean, Trudi," said Penelope. "Annie's at her best when mucking out and that sort of thing. She's very good at wheelbarrowing the smelly stuff."

"I wondered what was so stinky," said Trudi. "Yuck!" And she clasped her nose for dramatic effect.

Annie bit her lip and ignored them, deciding the best way to get rid of the Rainbow Sticky Foam was to give herself a shake.

"No!" cried Penelope. "Now it's all over the carpet. Mommy will be mad."

"Better get Annie to vacuum it up," said Trudi.

"No chance!"

"You do it, Trude," said Penelope. "Doing the Sticky Foam was your idea. I want to watch the ghost video. Spooky, spooky, *spooooky!*"

Bang! Bang! Bang! Something hammered against the TV room door.

"What's that?" said Penelope.

Nobody moved. Then Trudi, giggling nervously, tiptoed across the carpet and pulled the door open. Expecting something to burst in, Penelope crouched behind the sofa arm. Trudi looked in the hall.

"That's weird," she said. "We all heard the banging, didn't we? But there's no one there!"

Chapter 4

Spooks in the House

Only Annie saw the tiny chestnut pony canter across the carpet and push his way under the fringe on the side of the sofa. Her spirits lifted; Ned had come to her rescue. She kept a wary eye on the floor, wondering what he would do next. She took a deep breath.

"Wow! Spooks on the video, spooks in

the house." She raised her eyebrows and shrugged to make her point, guessing that Ned had become his big self and banged on the door before becoming tiny again. She was going to enjoy this. "Old houses often do have ghosts, don't they? I bet this house is old enough to have lots."

"Don't be stupid," said Penelope, getting up to look in the hall for herself.

"It was probably Pom Pom wanting to get in."

"Your mom took Pom Pom out for a walk. They were just going when I got here."

Penelope stared bleakly into the empty hall.

"It was the wind, then," said Trudi.

"Wind!" said Annie, crossing to the window. "There isn't even a teensy breeze outside today. Indoor *ghost* wind, maybe. Ghosts can make their own wind. I read it in a book, so it must be true."

From the corner of her eye Annie saw Ned canter out from the other end of the sofa and head for the remote control that lay on the carpet. Annie moved nearer to Penelope and Trudi to distract them if necessary. The pony reared up and brought his front feet down first on the volume button and then the play button.

The blast of sound surprised both

Trudi and Penelope, who clung to each other as *Hullabaloo and the Haunting of Flintstone Castle* blared unexpectedly from the television. Ned raced behind the curtains.

"Turn it off, turn it off!" shrieked Trudi.

Hiding a smile, Annie picked up the remote control.

"Hey, this is a good part," she said, watching Hullabaloo tiptoe down some dark stone stairs to a huge nail-studded door. He turned a giant key and the door creaked open. From deep in the gloomy dungeon, chains rattled ominously. Annie pressed the off button. "A really spooky video, just like you said, Penelope."

"How did it do it? How did the TV come on by itself?"

"I told you," said Annie. "You've got a ghost in the house. And watching ghost videos got it going. Seeing spooky friends has reminded it to get haunting."

"I don't believe in that kind of thing," said Trudi.

"Neither do I," said Penelope, but from her wide and staring eyes and the break in her voice, Annie could tell she was scared.

"What's that noise in the kitchen?" asked Annie, pretending to hear something.

Penelope looked startled. "What noise?"

"There wasn't a noise," said Trudi, marching into the hall to show how brave she was. Annie nodded.

"She's probably right. Let's face it, the ghost seems to be in here."

"I'll help Trudi check the kitchen," said Penelope, scurrying after her friend.

Annie closed the door and turned to find the curtains billowing as if something large was suddenly behind them.

"Ned," she whispered.

The pony's head pushed between the folds while his tail swished against the wallpaper. Now there was a full-sized pony in the TV room.

"Ned, they'll see you. Get tiny and let's go."

"Go!" replied Ned. "I don't think so. This is just starting to be fun. Quick,

Annie, get on." He burst from between the curtains, wearing his saddle and bridle. Voices in the hall made Annie hurry. She charged across the room, bounced across the sofa, and vaulted onto his back. As the door opened, there was a whirl of magic wind. Just in time, a tiny rider and tiny pony charged for the safety of the sofa fringe.

"She's gone," said Penelope.

"Good riddance," said Trudi and bounced across the sofa. "We can watch a video now."

"Not the haunting one," said Penelope. "I'm tired of ghosts."

Ned trotted out from the hiding place, and Annie looked up to see Trudi's elbow lean like a fallen tree trunk over the sofa's giant side. She just had time to straighten her riding hat before Ned set off at a canter for the hall.

"It's strange about Annie," said Penelope. "Disappearing like that."

"Oh, forget about her," said Trudi. "She can't take a joke — that's her trouble."

"You're right. No sense of humor."

Annie grinned, knowing she had a lot more of a sense of humor than Penelope imagined, and she stood in her stirrups while Ned cantered across the shiny floor to the bottom of the stairs.

"Hang on tight," he said. "We're going up. We've got some more haunting to do."

"But," Annie gasped, leaning into Ned's first jump, "aren't we going home?"

"Not yet," said Ned. "I think those two need a taste of their own medicine."

Annie didn't argue but concentrated on staying on. She didn't know how many stairs there were in Penelope's house, never having been up them before. When they arrived at the top, she was surprised by how long and wide the landing was.

"Which is Penelope's bedroom?" Ned asked.

"I don't know," whispered Annie. "What are you planning to do?"

"This," said Ned, and there was a whirl of wind and, to Annie's astonishment, they were their big selves again. Annie felt incredibly high up and exposed, riding a pony across the landing carpet. She looked over the banisters, half expecting to see Mrs. Potter in the hall and hear her scream and pass out with the shock. She was glad to be disguised by her magic riding clothes, in case it really happened.

"Ned, what if they see us?"

"They won't, and if they do they'll think we're ghosts. How else could a pony and rider be on the landing?"

Luckily, they didn't stay there for long; Ned wanted to find Penelope's bedroom.

"We need to find some ammunition," he said. "And then, before the haunting begins, you must go downstairs and join the others. That way, they can't say it was you."

Annie dismounted and let go of the reins. Instantly, her riding clothes vanished and, once she was back in ordinary clothes, her socks were good for tiptoeing. The first room they looked into was the bathroom. Ned poked his head around the door.

"We could do something with those."

"The toilet paper rolls?" There were three on a stand. "What, exactly?"

"You'll see. Bring them and that cap that's hanging from the faucet."

"The shower cap? What do you want with that?"

"I've got an idea."

They opened another door to find a room that was probably Mr. and Mrs. Potter's, for inside was a gigantic bed. The next room was certainly Penelope's. On a table by the window sat the new computer but, more impressive, a whole wall was covered with a multitude of bright ribbons and pictures of Penelope either standing with Pebbles, jumping Pebbles, trotting Pebbles, cantering Pebbles, or doing a lap of honor with Pebbles, a blue ribbon flying from his bridle.

"Look at that! Penelope's won so many!"

"Is that what you'd like?" Ned asked. "To win a blue ribbon?"

"More than anything in the world," replied Annie, and then she grinned a wicked grin. "Except maybe haunting." Ned wobbled his lips against a string bag full of tennis balls hanging on the back of the door. He turned to Annie.

"Well, haunting is what we will do," he said. Then he put his muzzle to her ear so he could whisper.

Chapter 5

This Ghost Rules!

The haunting preparations were quickly finished. Annie wore a mischievous smile as she hurried downstairs and tiptoed back to the TV room. She could hear the television blaring inside and, lifting her fist, she banged three times on the door. The effect was very satisfactory. Two loud squeals and two wide-eyed faces greeted her when she opened the door.

"Oh, it's you," said Penelope with obvious relief. "We thought you'd gone home."

"No," said Annie, leaving the door open behind her. "I went to find the bathroom."

"You've been gone for ages," said Trudi accusingly.

"I had trouble finding it." Annie sat on the end of the sofa. "Aren't you watching the ghost video?"

"We're watching *Dangerous Adventure* instead," said Trudi.

"Much more fun," added Penelope.

"Yes." Annie nodded. "Much better than ghosts. Hey, what was that?"

"What?" asked Penelope.

"It's that noise again." Annie grabbed

the remote control and turned down the volume. A steady clump-clumping echoed around the hall. "There, I told you. It's coming from upstairs. A sort of ghostly bumping."

Penelope eased herself up and crept to the open door. Annie and Trudi followed. At that precise moment, a red ribbon fluttered from between the banister rails

and landed on one of the rugs in the hall.
It was followed by a green one, a yellow, a
blue, and a mauve.

"Ribbons." Annie gasped. "Ghost
ribbons! Falling from nowhere!"

"Stop it, Annie," said Penelope. "You're scaring Trudi." But Annie could see that Penelope was pretty scared herself.

"It must be the wind," said Trudi. "It must be." Knowing it was Ned — hiding around the corner tossing ribbons with his teeth — Annie worked hard to keep a straight face.

"I don't think so," she said. "The wind would blow them up, not down. Definitely a ghost dropping them, I'd say."

Bump bump bump bump.
Down the stairs bounced
a roll of toilet paper,
unwinding to trail a
white streamer in its
wake.

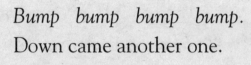

Bump bump bump bump.
Down came another one.

A third flew over
the banisters and
streamed all the
way to the front
door, like a wild
white bird.

Both Penelope and Trudi ducked and ended up crouching on the floor. There was a long silence when nothing happened. At last, Penelope stood up.

"Ha-ha! Very funny, Annie. You've done all this, haven't you? That's what you were doing when you were in the bathroom. Well, I'm not rolling up all that toilet paper. You can do it." And she bent to pick up a ribbon.

"Don't touch it," shrieked Trudi. "Look!" She pointed to the most terrifying thing of all, a white shower cap gliding in zigzags across the landing carpet. It turned in the most mysterious way, making one circle, then another, before speeding out of sight.

"I told you," Annie whispered, her expression deadly serious. Not in a million years would she let on that, underneath the shower cap, a tiny pony was galloping as fast as he could. "There *is* a ghost in the house. How could I possibly move a shower cap from down here?"

Penelope and Trudi looked at each other in terror. First one, then the other, ran screaming toward the kitchen door.

"Get rid of it," yelled Penelope. "Get rid of it." The big Ned quickly leaned over the banister and lobbed a couple of tennis balls at their retreating backs, causing more screams before the door banged shut and the commotion faded into the distance.

"Hurry up, Ned," said Annie. "We've got to get out of here before they come back."

"They won't come back. They'll be hiding in the yard by now," he said. "But Mrs. Potter could arrive at any minute. Quick. Come and get on."

Annie leaped over the trail of toilet paper and raced upstairs. With another vault, she was astride the pony. The magic wind blew, and they became a tiny pony and tiny rider, galloping for the stairs. Down they went, jump stride jump

stride jump, with Annie counting steps all the way to the bottom.

Now, with miles of hall floor before them, Ned raced for the kitchen door, leaping over the toilet paper streamers and any ribbons in their path, galloping across a rug patterned with leaves and flowers that stretched ahead like a six-acre field. The speed was tremendous, and the whistling wind brought tears to Annie's eyes.

At last, the brown panels of the kitchen door loomed above them.

"I'll have to get off and open it," cried Annie.

"No, wait!" panted Ned, skidding to a halt by the door frame. "Someone's coming." Footsteps stopped on the other side, and the door opened. It was Mrs. Potter. Ned dodged around her tree-trunk legs and sped into the kitchen.

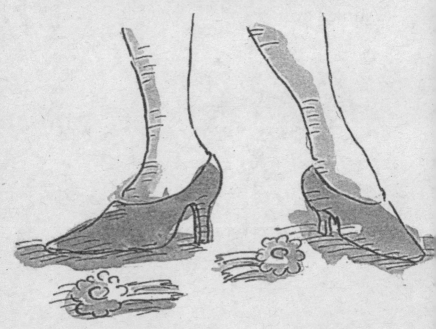

Behind them, Mrs. Potter discovered the mess in the hall and gave a cry of dismay; in front, they heard a growl. Pom Pom bent toward them, eyes like glinting coal, his top lip curling above a row of ivory teeth. The growl rumbled on until Ned reared high, tumbling Annie into the magic wind so that she landed with a mighty bump at her correct size. Pom Pom yelped with surprise and ran under the table to hide.

"Good gracious, Annie. What are you doing down there?" Mrs. Potter demanded. "And what do you know about this mess in the hall?"

Sitting on the floor, Annie turned up frightened eyes.

"I . . . I . . ." Nothing would come out. She looked around for Ned.

"Goodness, Annie, don't tell me you're going to say there's a ghost in the house, too?" said Mrs. Potter, clasping Annie's arm and hauling her up.

"There *is* a ghost," cried Annie, thinking this would be the best way to explain her confused state. "It's really freaky."

Mrs. Potter brushed her off. From the corner of her eye, Annie saw Ned gallop out the back door. From under the table, Pom Pom saw him, too, but having just missed being flattened, he was staying put.

"It's all silly nonsense, Annie. I'm surprised at you," said Mrs. Potter. "Pom Pom — what are you doing under the table? Naughty dog. Get in your bed." But Pom Pom wouldn't budge.

"I have to go," said Annie, leaving Mrs. Potter to pull the unwilling dog out alone. She darted into the utility room in time to see Ned leap into the yard and take cover behind a flowerpot. Annie breathed a sigh of relief and pulled on her boots. Ned was safe.

Outside, Penelope and Trudi waited anxiously in the courtyard.

"Is the ghost gone?" called Penelope.

"We're not coming in until it is," said Trudi.

"Don't ask me," said Annie. "It might have. Then again, it might still be lurking." Mrs. Potter arrived at the doorstep and Annie made a run for it.

"Penelope, Trudi, come in at once. I suppose all this talk of a ghost in the house is an excuse for the disgraceful mess in the hall. I want it cleaned up at once."

Annie hurried to escape, wondering how long it would take Mrs. Potter to persuade them to go in — and how long it would take Penelope and Trudi to clean up.

When she reached the gate at the bottom of the drive, Mr. Potter drove in on his way back from the supermarket.

"Going already, Annie?" he said. "Here." And he reached over into a cooler. "Your Wally Whizzer. You can't go without that."

"Oh, thank you," said Annie. "Thanks very much."

With a wave, Mr. Potter drove on.

The gate to Penelope's stable yard was open and a low whicker came from behind the hedge. Annie darted across the street to find the big Ned hiding in the yard.

"Thank goodness you're safe. I thought Pom Pom was going to eat you."

"It would take more than a yappy poodle to do that," said Ned cheerfully. "So that's a Wally Whizzer Wonderstick Ice Cream, is it?"

"Yes, would you like some?" Annie asked, pulling off the wrapper, which she stuffed into her pocket. "It's chocolate and vanilla ice cream and has a fruity surprise in the middle."

"Sounds delicious." Annie held out a piece for Ned to try. "It is delicious."

When the Wally Whizzer was finished, Annie put the stick and the paper in the tack room's garbage can. When she returned, Ned was wearing his saddle and bridle.

"There's still time for a ride in Winchway Wood," he said.

"A ride," said Annie. "Yes, please!" She put her foot in the stirrup and leaped onto his back. Instantly, she was dressed in the magic riding clothes, her perfect disguise. Annie shut the gate behind them and Ned trotted down the road past Mrs. Plumley's house and Annie's house and on toward the wood.

"A walk, a trot, a canter, a gallop, a leap or two over the fallen log, and home again," said Ned, which is just what they did. Annie loved every minute of it — the trees rushing past as Ned galloped up

the path, the sense of togetherness as they jumped the log, and the sheer exhilaration of knowing how much better her riding had become since Ned had been teaching her. By the time they arrived back at the front gate, Annie was glowing with happiness.

"Thank you, Ned. That was a wonderful ride," she said.

"I'm glad you enjoyed it. And now it's time for me to return to my poster."

Her bedroom window was still open and Annie guessed which way Ned would go. The large leaves of the fig tree made the perfect staircase up to her windowsill. She slid to the ground, took a last look at her beloved magic riding clothes, and let go of the reins.

Back in her jeans and sweatshirt, Annie watched the big Ned disappear and the tiny Ned trot around in front of

her. She bent down, held out flat palms,
and up he jumped. Pushing open the
front gate with her bottom, she
carried the tiny pony to
the fig tree and watched
while he leaped from
leaf to leaf all the way
up to her bedroom.
Then Annie hurried around the house to
the back door.

She found Dad in the kitchen, staring
at a piece of burned toast in the toaster.
She pulled off her rubber boots.

"Still not working?"

"Not quite. Did you take care of Pebbles, and is Penelope better?"

"I did, and Penelope is better."

"Good," said Dad, turning back to the toaster.

Annie hurried upstairs to her bedroom. Tabitha lay curled up on her bed and Ned gazed down from his poster. She wished the magic hadn't ended; now she would have to wait until next time.

She checked to see Pebbles grazing happily in his field on the other side of the road and closed the window. Spinning around, she dived onto her bed.

"Tabs, guess what?" Tabitha woke up and stretched. "Ned's been a ghost. It was great. And we had a fantastic ride in the woods. And something else — Penelope's got hundreds of ribbons on her wall." She looked up at the chestnut pony in the poster.

"Maybe one day I'll win a blue ribbon. With a magic pony, anything can happen!"

Magic Pony

Join Annie and Ned
on their next adventure!

Nighttime is the best time
to practice jumps!

Annie woke up suddenly and unexpectedly. Something in the dark was tickling her ear. It felt like the hairy feet of a spider and she quickly brushed it away. The tickling started again on her chin and warm air blew on her cheek. Pressing herself against the wall, she reached the light switch at last. She laughed when the light came on. It wasn't a spider at all. Not even close. It was the tickling of pony whiskers and the blowing of warm pony breath. Ned, the beautiful chestnut pony who lived in the poster pinned to her bedroom wall, had wakened her. His gentle lips nuzzled affectionately against her cheek. How lucky she was to have such a secret: her very own magic pony. She rubbed the sleep from her eyes and glanced at the clock on the shelf.

"Hello," said the pony cheerfully, not seeming to mind that he only just fit into the space between the bed and the wall.

"Ned," said Annie. "It's two-thirty in the morning. Why aren't you asleep?"

"Now what sort of greeting is that?" asked the pony. "Do you want me to go back in my poster?"

"No," said Annie, alarmed that he might. Ever since buying this most unusual pony poster from Cosby's Magic Emporium, Annie never quite knew when Ned would come alive. If the magic was happening now, she didn't want to waste a moment of it. "It's only that it's the middle of the night. I've never been awake at two-thirty in the morning before."

"That's the whole point," said Ned. "Everyone in the house is fast asleep, even that cat."

Ned meant Tabitha, Annie's tabby cat, who lay curled up on the bed. This wasn't quite true, for Annie's wriggling had disturbed her, and Tabitha had half an eye open. As for Ned, whether big or small — and he could be either — Tabitha had learned to ignore him.

"It's the perfect time for jumping practice. So get up and get on."

During the day, when her curtains were open, Annie often watched Penelope Potter jump her pony, Pebbles, over the blue barrels in the field on the other side of the road. And now Ned was teaching her to do the same! What did it matter if it was the middle of the night? Annie scrambled out from under the covers, leaving Tabitha to curl up into an undisturbed ball.

"I can't ride in pajamas. I'd better get my jeans on."

"No need for that," said Ned. And of course there wasn't, for the moment Annie sat on Ned's back, the magic would change her pajamas into riding clothes.

"Where shall we jump?" Annie asked, putting her bare toes into the waiting stirrup and springing on. The pony's reply was drowned out in a rushing wind, and Annie closed her eyes. When she opened them again, Ned was trotting across a field of brown tufts that Annie recognized as her carpet. Ned's magic had shrunk them into the tiniest pony and tiniest rider in the world. He rounded the towering height of the door and cantered toward the top of the stairs, guided by the light that spilled from Annie's bedroom.

"Where are we going?" Annie whispered.

"Downstairs, of course," came the reply.

The drop from the landing onto the first stair was huge and the giant steps disappeared into a pit of black. Jumping practice was starting in earnest. Annie clung on, remembering she had gone downstairs like this before. By the time they reached the hall, Annie's eyes were staring pools, desperate to fathom what lay ahead in the darkness. To her relief, she hadn't fallen off. Just as well! Any loud noise would wake Mom, Dad, and Jamie, and she certainly didn't want that.

"Get off now," said Ned. "And switch on the dining room light. We'll set up a jumping course in there."

"Oh, yes," said Annie. "I know the very best place." She slid to the ground and let go of the reins. The wind spun her until she was her correct size and back in her pajamas. She tiptoed forward, following the tiny Ned. He cantered in front of her as if he were Esmerelda, Prince, or Percy, one of her three china horses, come to life. She pushed open the dining room door and switched on the light. Fred, the goldfish, fluttered into action in his bowl on the shelf, surprised by the sudden brightness. Annie hurried to the table. It was already set for breakfast, just the way Mom liked it.

"Ned, let's make a jumping course up here. There's lots of things that could be jumps."

"Show me." Annie held out her hand and lifted him. Ned was soon trotting across the tablecloth, inspecting the breakfast dishes.

"Yes," he said. "The syrup bottle, the knives and forks, and the salt and pepper shakers. We can use all those."

"And the mugs," said Annie. "They can lie on their sides and be pretend barrels. Almost as good as the barrels Penelope Potter has for Pebbles to jump."

"They'll make a mighty jump, mind you," said Ned, trotting around one. "The plates are no use. They need to be put off to one side."

"My schoolbag's here," said Annie

grabbing it from beside a chair and diving in. "My pens and pencils can be poles."

She scattered three felt-tips and two striped pencils on the table and pulled out her scissors. "What can my scissors be? I know, they can be opened out and balanced on their handles. They're not sharp, so there's no chance of getting cut. They'll make a great cross-blade jump. And look, Mom's sewing basket is loaded with spools of thread. They can be jump stands."

"Good thinking," said Ned. "As our small selves we'll practice indoors on the table, and as our large selves we'll ride out to Penelope Potter's field and jump Pebbles's barrels."

"In the dark?" exclaimed Annie, already

balancing a knife and a fork across the salt and pepper shakers.

"It's a full moon tonight," said Ned. "With luck, we'll have plenty of light."

Annie darted to the window and pulled back the curtains, knowing Penelope would hate someone else jumping her blue barrels, even if it was in the dark. So she wouldn't find out. Annie shielded her eyes and looked into the garden. Through a gap in the ballooning clouds, a round moon flooded silver light across the grass.

"If the clouds clear away, it'll be perfect," Annie said, looking for stars. How exciting it would be to do nighttime jumping outdoors. She returned to the table.

After the salt-and-pepper shaker–knife-

and-fork jump, she opened the scissors and balanced them on their handles to make the cross-blade jump. The mugs were put on their sides and turned into barrels, and the spools of thread were stacked at three different heights. Two of the pens and one of the pencils became poles, making the pen and pencil staircase.

Next she turned the syrup bottle on its side to make a wall. And finally, Annie discovered Mom's glasses in the sewing basket, opened them out, and made three jumps. The eyeglasses single, if jumped facing the lenses, or the eyeglasses double, if the arms were jumped. She bounced over them with her fingers — *boing! boing!* Then she watched enchanted as Ned, mane flying, jumped the whole course.

It was a clear round and Annie clasped her hands to stop herself from clapping — a thing certain to wake the family and bring them downstairs to find out what was going on. Instead, her delight was shown by a grin that grew wider and wider as Ned trotted toward her. Leaning back on his haunches, he bowed politely.

"Now it's your turn, Annie. I'll come down to the floor, then you can mount. But we'll need some sort of road to ride up, to get us back up here as our small selves."

"I know," said Annie. "If I pull Dad's chair close to the table, we can use the rug."

She hurried to show Ned what she meant. After a bit of a struggle, she had the chair in position with the rug draped over it. One end hung from the chair back while Annie stretched the other end out over the seat and weighted it with the legs of the small table. Now there was a long ramp from the floor to the top of the chair.

"Well done," said Ned, impressed. He jumped onto the rug and galloped all the way down to the floor without causing the slightest sag.

When his feet touched the floor, he was suddenly his big self, wearing saddle and bridle and filling a large part of the room. Annie squeezed between Ned and the table and took hold of the reins.

The moment she sprang into the saddle, the mighty wind blew. When it stopped, she was dressed in her magic riding clothes and was dwarfed by giant furniture. As she looked up, her breath was taken away by the vast chair and rug mountain. Ned stepped onto the rug ramp cautiously, but Annie's extra weight made no difference; the rug stayed taut and stretched. The pony trotted briskly all the way to the top and jumped onto the table.

Annie gasped with surprise at what she saw. As her big self she thought she had made the show jumps sensibly low, but now that she was a tiny rider they looked huge. Most frightening of all were the giant mug barrels — imposingly round and solid and higher than Ned's shoulders.

"This is just the sort of practice course you need," said Ned. "Jump all of these and you'll soon be showing that Penelope Potter what's what."

There's Magic in Every Book!

The Rainbow Fairies
Books #1-7

The Weather Fairies
Books #1-7

The Jewel Fairies
Books #1-7

The Pet Fairies
Books #1-7

The Fun Day Fairies
Books #1-7

SCHOLASTIC
www.scholastic.com
www.rainbowmagiconline.com

HiT entertainment

FAIRYG

How can one Pet cause so much Trouble?

Runaway Retriever

Loudest Beagle on the Block

Mud-Puddle Poodle

Bulldog Won't Budge

Oh No, Newf!

Smarty-Pants Sheltie

Bad to the Bone Boxer

Dachshund Disaster

Read the series and find out!